WATERSHIP DOWN

First published in paperback, 2019 by Macmillan Children's Books
an imprint of Pan Macmillan
20 New Wharf Road, London N1 9RR
Associated companies throughout the world
www.panmacmillan.com

ISBN: 978-1-5098-8164-2

A CIP catalogue record for this book is available
from the British Library

Printed in Italy

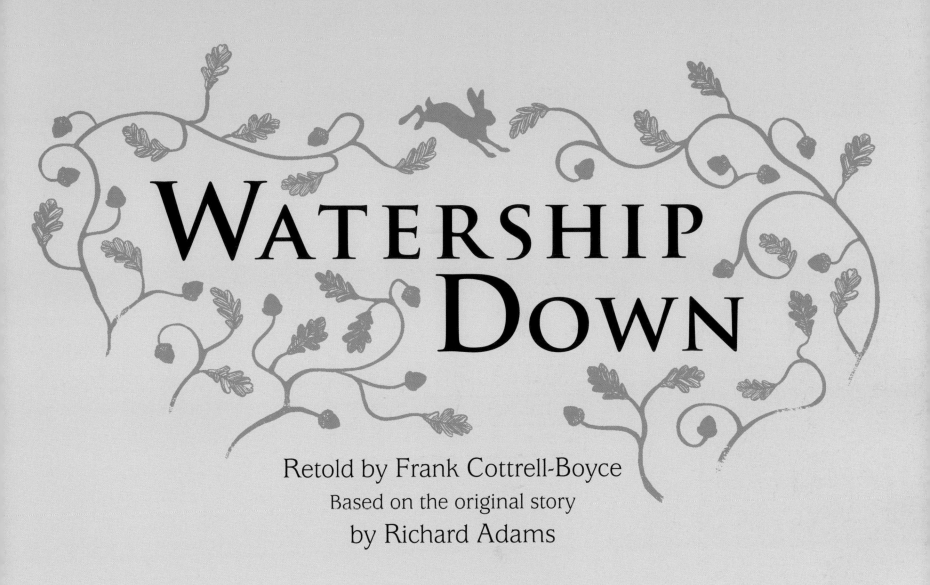

WATERSHIP DOWN

Retold by Frank Cottrell-Boyce

Based on the original story

by Richard Adams

MACMILLAN CHILDREN'S BOOKS

GLOSSARY

The Owsla - the strongest rabbits in a warren, who rule over the others

Hrududu - a tractor, car or other motor vehicle

Silflay - to go above ground to feed

Flay-rah - treats that wild rabbits don't usually get, such as carrots and lettuce

Elil - enemies of rabbits

Efrafa - the warren founded by General Woundwort

CHARACTERS

Frith
The sun-god and
creator of the
universe

Threarah
Chief rabbit of
the Sandleford
Warren

El-ahrairah
The rabbit folk
hero, smart,
devious and tricky

Bigwig
Formerly a member
of the Sandleford
Owsla, now one of
Hazel's supporters

Bluebell
A survivor of the
destruction of
Sandleford Warren
– a natural storyteller

Hazel
One of the leaders
of the Sandleford
rabbits

Fiver
Hazel's younger
brother

Cowslip
A member of a
strange warren
– he invites the
Sandleford rabbits
to join him

Strawberry
A member of another
warren, who asks to
join the Sandleford
rabbits

Kehaar
An injured seagull
who is befriended
by Hazel

*General
Woundwort*
Chief Rabbit of
Efrafa, a fearless and
tyrannical leader

*The Black
Rabbit of Inlé*
A phantom rabbit who
appears when death
is near

"Tell us a story, Bluebell."

"Yes, a story!"

"A new one though. One we've never heard before . . ."

At the beginning of the world, Frith, creator of the world, saw that rabbits were eating all the food.

So he gave teeth to the foxes,
and claws to the hawks and
told them to hunt the rabbits.

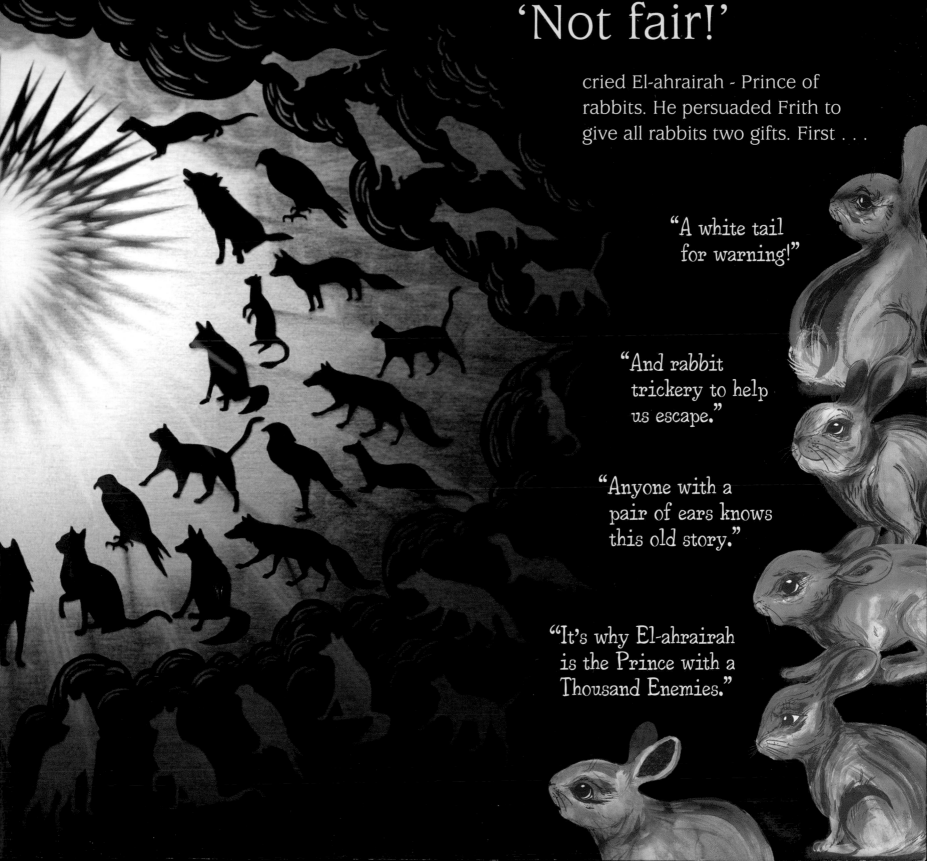

'Not fair!'

cried El-ahrairah - Prince of
rabbits. He persuaded Frith to
give all rabbits two gifts. First . . .

"A white tail
for warning!"

"And rabbit
trickery to help
us escape."

"Anyone with a
pair of ears knows
this old story."

"It's why El-ahrairah
is the Prince with a
Thousand Enemies."

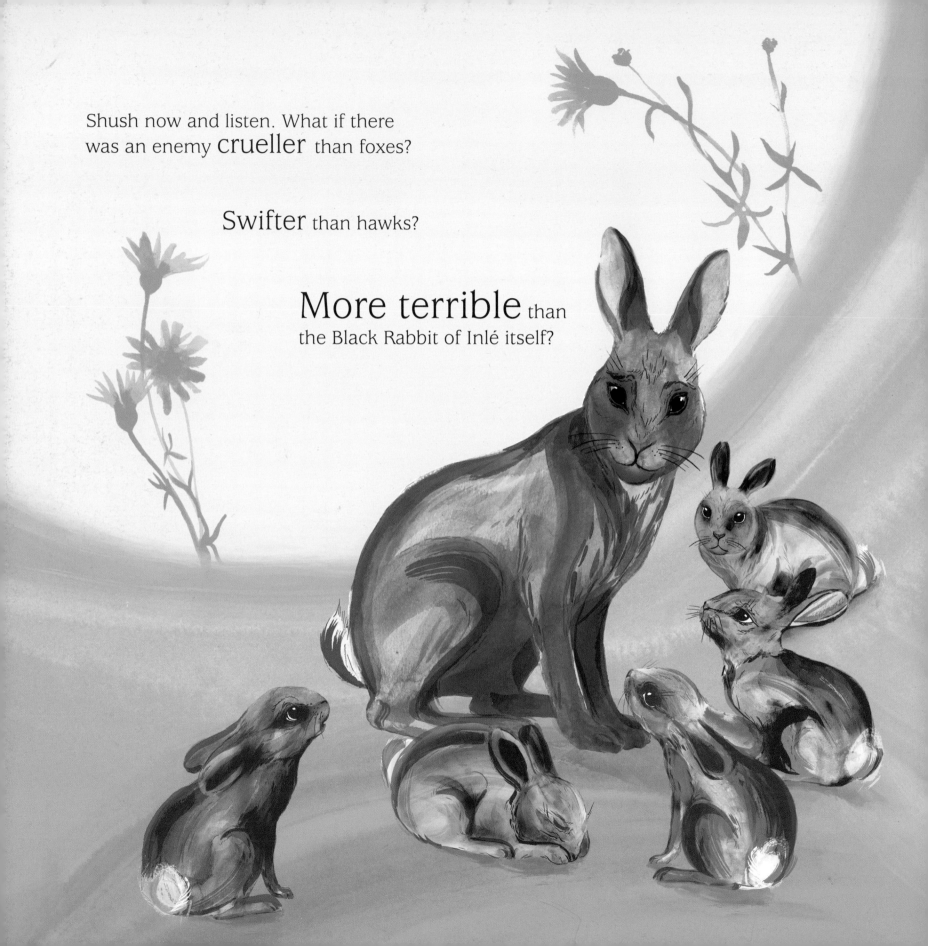

Shush now and listen. What if there was an enemy **crueller** than foxes?

Swifter than hawks?

More terrible than the Black Rabbit of Inlé itself?

This is the story of how Hazel-rah and his little band defeated an elil that was greater than all the thousand enemies, and discovered a something stronger even than our Frith-given tricks and tails.

In a faraway warren called Sandleford, a fierce Threarah and his Owsla kept watch over all the rabbits.

But one young rabbit, Fiver, had a dream. In this dream he saw the warren covered in blood.

'It must be a warning,' he said to his brother Hazel. 'Some terrible thing is coming.'

Brave Hazel went to the Threarah and said, 'We must all flee.'

'Frith in a pond!' laughed the Threarah. 'Is your brother mad? What kind of fool would leave home and safety because of a dream?'

He told his Owsla to let no one leave the warren.

But Hazel believed in Fiver. That night in secret,
they gathered a few friends and fled.

One member of the Owsla, a great warrior Bigwig,
heard their story and decided to join them.

All night

the Owsla

hunted

them.

But they escaped from the warren and began their terrible journey. How did they travel through the pitch-dark wood?

"They followed each other's tails!"

When a conspiracy of ravens chased them for daring to enter their cathedral, how did they get away?

"Used their rabbit tricks!"

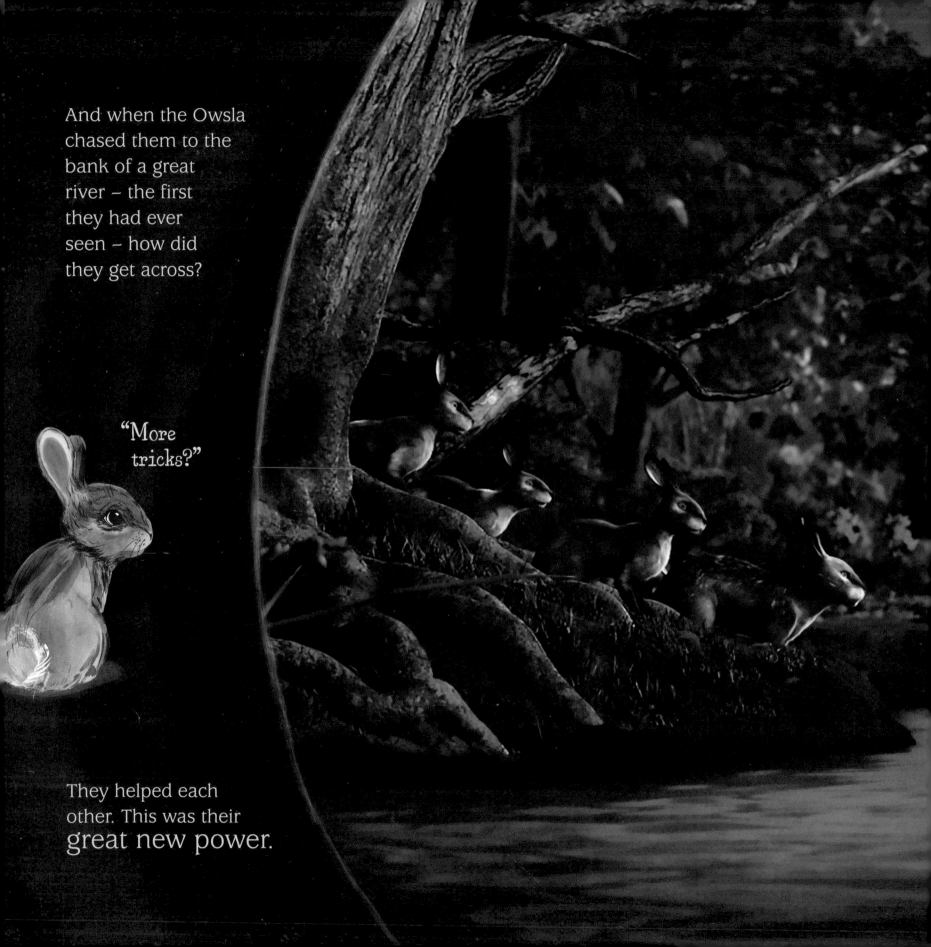

And when the Owsla
chased them to the
bank of a great
river – the first
they had ever
seen – how did
they get across?

"More
tricks?"

They helped each
other. This was their
great new power.

They were not the **strongest** rabbits.

Or the **trickiest**. They were all **afraid**.

But they **believed** in each other.

"That's nice."

Sometimes Hazel thought he saw the Black Rabbit of Inlé following them, but he never told the others so they would not be scared.

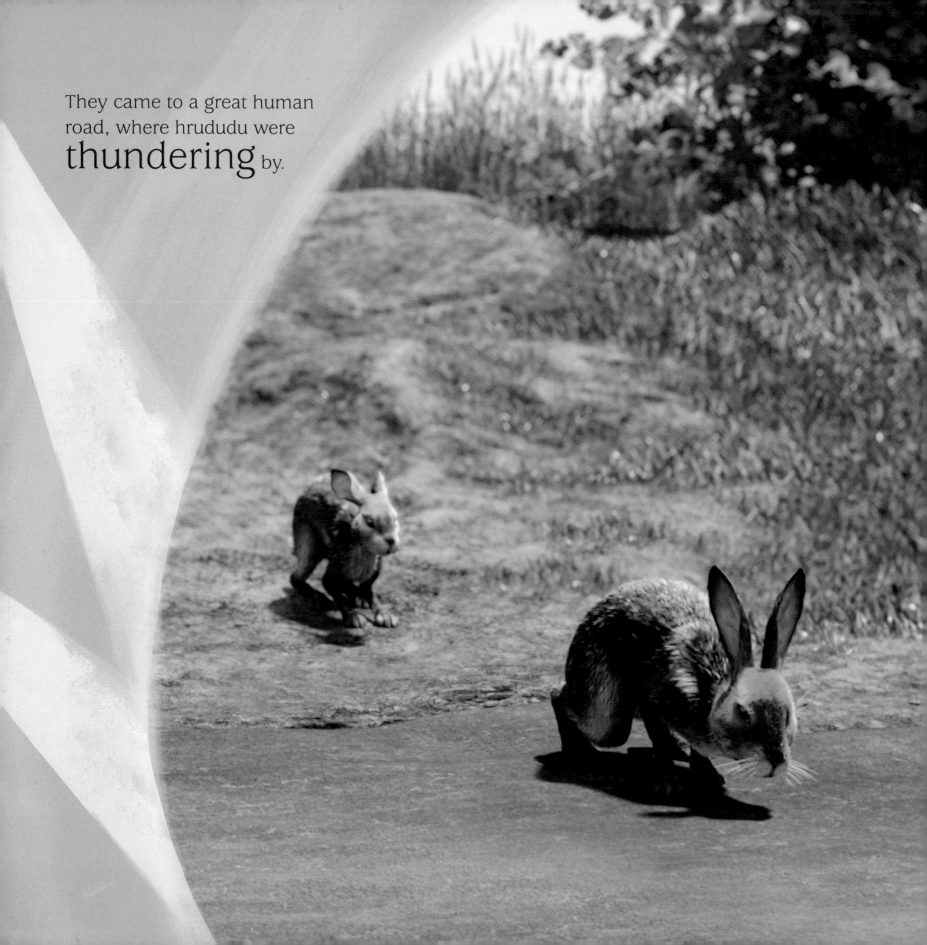

They came to a great human road, where hrududu were **thundering** by.

Bigwig led them
safely across.

'We're cold and hungry
and we don't know how
to dig burrows,' said Bigwig.
'We should have stayed
in Sandleford.'

But just then a stranger
rabbit appeared. 'You can
come to our warren,' he said.
'We have plenty of room.
My name is Cowslip.'

Fiver was **suspicious**.
Rabbits never invite
strangers into their warren.

Then Cowslip said,
'. . . and we have flay-rah!'

"Oh, I love flay-rah!"

Cowslip's warren was huge.
And so were the rabbits
who lived there —

'Oh brambles!' said Hazel.
'They are so strong and well fed.
This must be a good place.'

In the heart of the warren was
a great domed room.
The Sandleford rabbits had
never seen anything so
beautiful. But Fiver dreamed
again, and in his dream he saw
a dome made all of bones.

One evening while he was out at **silflay**, Bigwig's neck was caught in a **snare.**

The stranger rabbits ran away, but Hazel and his little band managed to free Bigwig . . .

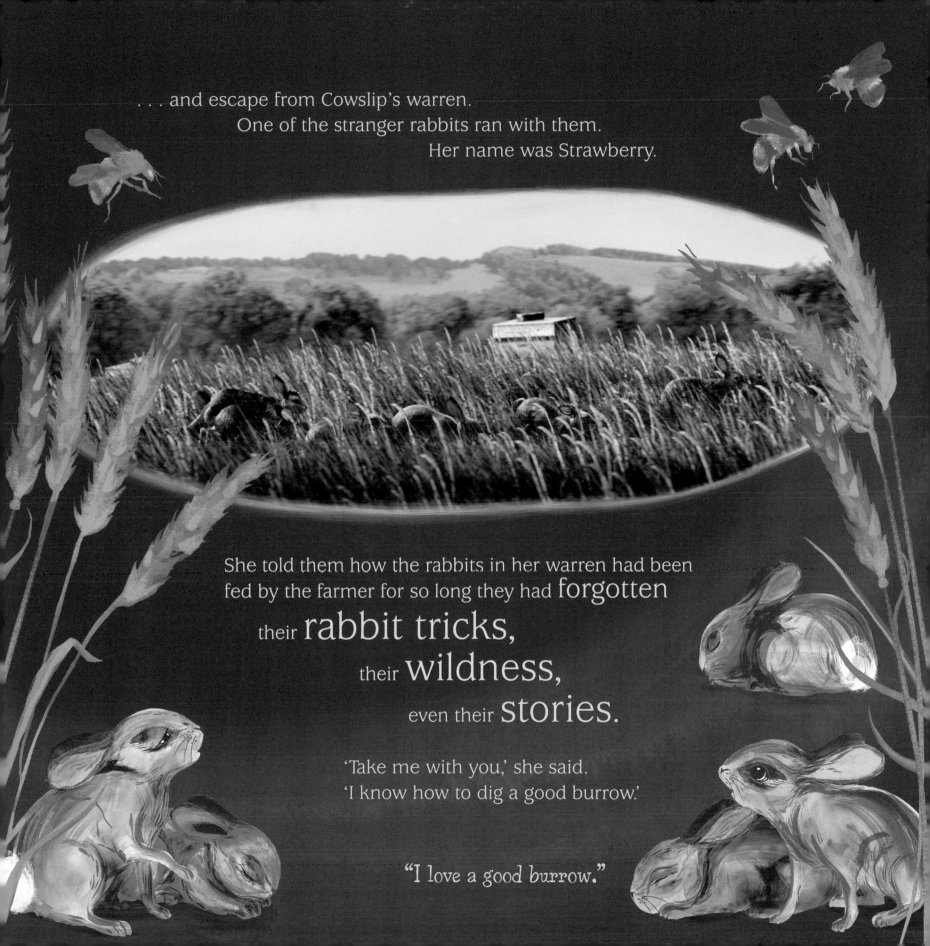

. . . and escape from Cowslip's warren.
One of the stranger rabbits ran with them.
Her name was Strawberry.

She told them how the rabbits in her warren had been
fed by the farmer for so long they had forgotten

their rabbit tricks,

their wildness,

even their stories.

'Take me with you,' she said.
'I know how to dig a good burrow.'

"I love a good burrow."

They journeyed on.

In a barn they saw a **terrible**
sight – rabbits kept in cages,
begging to be set free.
'We want to see the sky,'
they cried. A dog and a cat
came and chased Hazel and
his band away before
they could do anything.

They ran and ran until
they came to a hill with a
great spreading tree.

"Like home?"

The very same. That was
Watership Down.

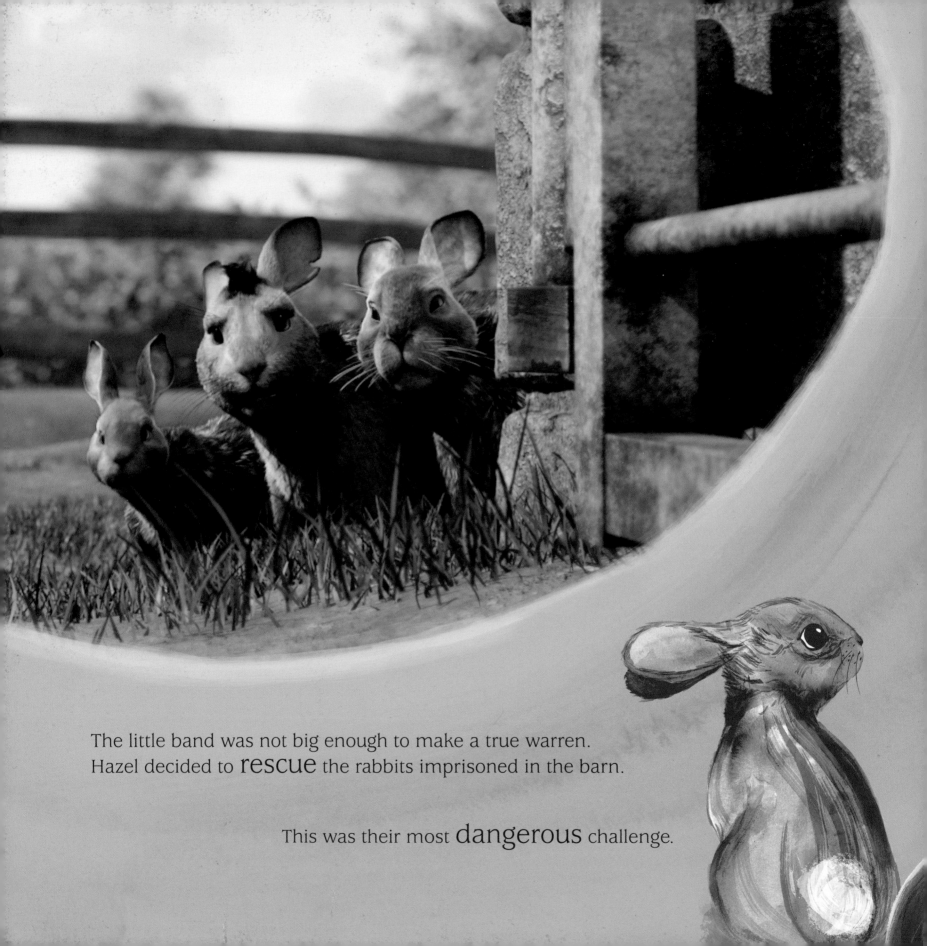

The little band was not big enough to make a true warren.
Hazel decided to **rescue** the rabbits imprisoned in the barn.

This was their most **dangerous** challenge.

But as he led the prisoner-rabbits
to freedom, Hazel saw that
someone was following him;

. . . the Black Rabbit of Inlé.

'Hazel,' she called.

'I've followed you this far.

Run away now
but I will catch you one day.'

Up on Watership Down the rabbits had no fear. 'We can see for miles,' said Bigwig. 'No enemy will be able to get near us.'

As he said this, a shadow fell over him. A great bird crashed into the hill. The bird was hurt. They fed him and cared for him.

"But birds are elil!"

Sometimes. But Hazel and his band had learned that fear is a useful servant but a terrible master. This bird was named Kehaar.

"Like Kehaar our friend!"

This was that very same Kehaar. He was younger then. As soon as his wings were mended, he flew over the hills and told the rabbits what he had seen.

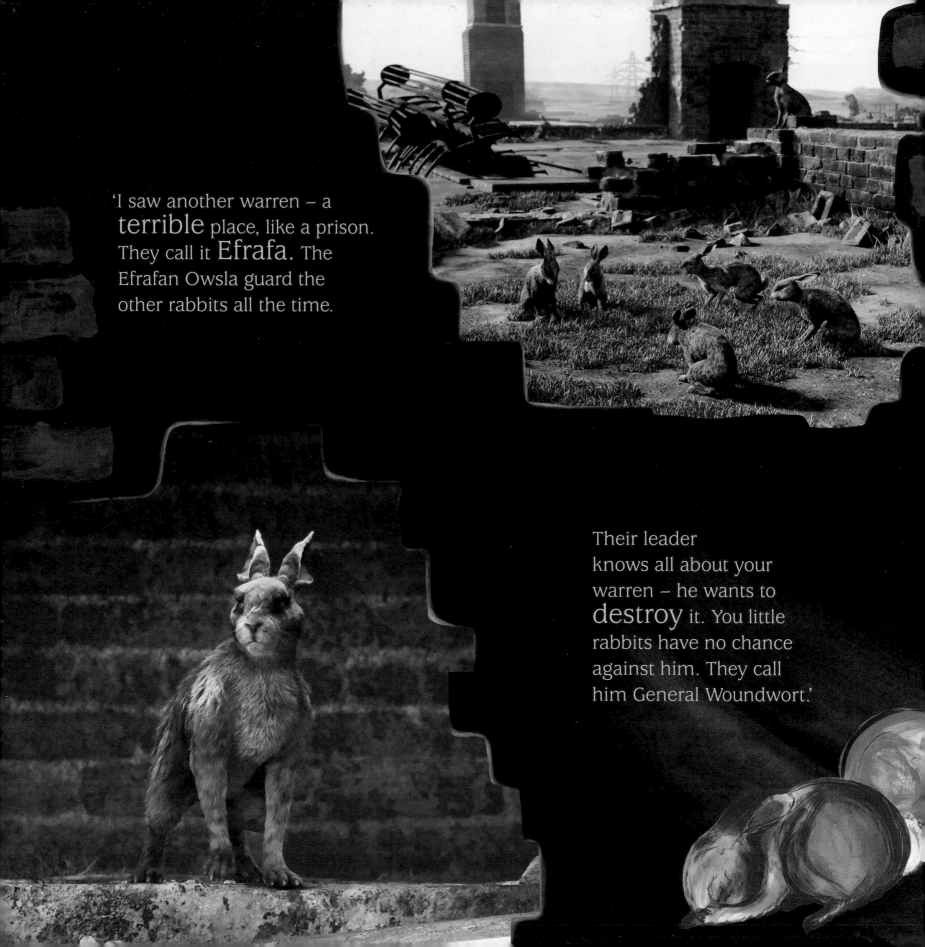

'I saw another warren – a **terrible** place, like a prison. They call it **Efrafa**. The Efrafan Owsla guard the other rabbits all the time.

Their leader knows all about your warren – he wants to **destroy** it. You little rabbits have no chance against him. They call him General Woundwort.'

Bigwig went to Efrafa to see if any of the rabbits wanted to leave with him. But the Efrafan Owsla would not let him leave.

"I'm scared now!"

Then listen.

That night, when Bigwig did
not return, Fiver dreamed a
great rabbit trick.
Hazel led a group of rabbits to
the farm. They teased the farm dog.

When it chased them they led it
into the midst of Woundwort's
forces there on Watership Down.

General Woundwort was killed.

The trick had been clever but dangerous too. Weary and bruised, Hazel lay down. Someone was coming towards him.

The Black Rabbit of Inlé.

But now Hazel had learned not to be afraid. Instead of running away he went with the Black Rabbit.

'The rabbits of Watership Down
will be safe now,' said the
Black Rabbit, 'for they
have their tricks
and they have their
white tails …

. . . and most of all, they **care for each other.** So fear will never be their master.'